D1480030

Every morning, Old McGinty woke up before it was light and picked his way down the stony trail from his house to the sea.

Every morning, he greeted his fishing dory, the *Heart's Content*. "Good morning, my girl," and he shoved the yellowed stern out into the salty spray.

And every day for over sixty years, the old boat and the old man caught fathoms of fish.

Until one morning, there was hardly a nibble.

"Where are the fish?" McGinty asked the *Heart's Content.*

He rowed way, way out into the bay. He heaved the sodden net overboard and then stood at the prow of his boat. For luck, he belted out two songs: *"Oh Can-a-da,"* and then his very own, very proud version *"Oh New-found-land."*

When the sun was low in the sky, he pulled in the gillnet, hand over hand over hand. Only a few slippery fish sluiced into the bottom of the boat.

McGinty rowed back and beached the *Heart's Content.* He collected some driftwood, built a fire, and boiled a codfish for breakfast. The blackened teapot burbled on the coals.

"Ahh…," he sighed, and he said a little prayer of thanks to God, to Canada, and to Newfoundland.

But the next day, when McGinty rowed out, he caught no fish at all. And he had no real breakfast.

The next day he rowed further.

No fish. No breakfast!

"My stomach is growling," McGinty said to the *Heart's Content*.
"How are you feeling, m'dear?"
The boat pressed on.
Day after day. Week after week. He rowed further and still no fish. Just one tiny flounder that he threw back into the sea.
McGinty pulled the *Heart's Content* out of the water, left her resting on the rocks. Turtled.

Now, every other night, McGinty's telephone rang at precisely nine o'clock.

"That'll be the granddaughter…Luv'ly to hear from you, Molly!" He closed his eyes and waited for the dreaded question.

"Move to Vancouver Island?" he asked. "Ridiculous! Molly…Molly…I don't care if they are catching fish as big as cows in Cowichan Bay. My home is here. You're not to worry. I have *so* been catching fish. I miss you too, my love."

McGinty could not sleep. He put on his red corduroy slippers and his plaid wool robe and scuffled down the stony trail to talk to the *Heart's Content*.

McGinty paced up and down. "I am hungry," he said. "And look at you, my girl — you're peeling and drying out."

He sat on a rock. "You are old and I am old. We have been together a long time. What shall we do?"

"I did have one little idea I've been keeping from you." McGinty pulled out the globe hidden under his bathrobe. "I want to discuss it." He spun the world around and measured the distance from St. John's, Newfoundland, to Victoria, British Columbia, with the span of his great hand.

"It's not so far, ten inches is all. We can do it. We must do it. We need to fish!" McGinty sent a telegram to his granddaughter:

GOING ON A LONG LONG VOYAGE STOP
WILL CALL WHEN I DOCK STOP

Then McGinty telephoned the train station on the mainland.

He boarded up the house. He scraped the traces of barnacles off the *Heart's Content*. He rubbed her and painted her until she gleamed. He mounted a compass in the bow. "You're going on a long and tremendous voyage," said McGinty. "We must make you sound."

McGinty flew directly to Toronto and stayed in the only hotel he knew. He looked out the window with his spyglass, waiting for the *Heart's Content*.

Every evening, he telephoned the train station.

"Is she here yet?" he asked the stationmaster. "What's her position, laddie?" He charted her course on the map he'd tacked to the hotel room wall.

By the fifth day, McGinty was in great distress. "Is she lost? At sea? We've never been apart — I must set eyes on her!"

"It's against the rules," growled the stationmaster. Then he whispered, "She departs Toronto tonight."

Old McGinty checked out of the hotel. He bought a sleeping bag, some warm woollen socks, red flannel underwear, fresh water, and a case of canned mackerel.

He hurried to the rail terminal. He limped along the gravel of Track Number Three as fast as his land legs would take him. Past rail cars of coal and plywood. Coils of steel. Giant rolls of newsprint.

He crossed to Track Two and searched from caboose to engine. No boat.

"Where are you, girl?" Then he spied her, sidelined all alone.

McGinty walked away, and then turned back. "I know this is the first time you and I have been apart, but I cannot go with you. You are freight and I'm a passenger. You'll be fine on that train. Don't be afraid."

He knelt down, filled the old teapot to the brim with Atlantic sea water, and set it gently in the bottom of the *Heart's Content*.

McGinty blew his nose on his white handkerchief and cleared his throat. "I will wait for you half way, m'dear — if that would be quite all right with you."

He patted the *Heart's Content* and wished her good day and good luck.

One last time, McGinty picked his way along the stony trail from his house to the sea. As the sun was setting over the bay at Come-by-Chance, McGinty sang only one song: *"Ode to Newfoundland."*

McGinty removed his cap and bowed low from the waist. "Good evening, m'dear," he said to the *Heart's Content*. "My, my — you're drier than a salt cod." He sprinkled some water from the old teapot onto her hull, and rubbed it in.

Then, McGinty quietly, stealthily, stowed away his gear — and himself!

He braced his feet on the port gunwale and rested his head on a lifebuoy at starboard. He battened down the tarpaulin.

"Snug as a bug in a rug!" said McGinty.

Stowaway McGinty turned night into day.

He straddled the prow of his ship and navigated by the stars. He watched the
endless shadows of forest roll past.

The moon was low in the sky, shining across the islands of Lake Superior.
The Northern Lights shivered in the heavens and on the water.

Across the Prairies, he poked up his head like a gopher, and rowed the waves of golden grain.

Up and over, up and over the ripples of the Alberta foothills.

"Brace y'self, missy," warned Captain McGinty. "There's heavy weather ahead."

And sure enough, the *Heart's Content* bobbed and bounced through the heave and ho of the Rocky Mountains…

…over the Fraser Canyon…

…and came to rest, shunted at the Strait of Georgia.

"Almost there, m'girl," whispered Captain McGinty. "Can you taste the salt of the Pacific Ocean?"

The *Heart's Content* rolled onto a ferry bound for Vancouver Island.

On this last leg of the voyage, Captain McGinty threw back the tarpaulin. "Whales to the portside!" he called happily. "Sea otters and seals north by northwest. Land Ho-*oh*!"

Captain McGinty watched eagerly as the *Heart's Content* was lowered into the water. He took an oar and splashed her until she was slippery and shining.

He pulled on his sou'wester and his big rubber boots and out from his pockets came maps and charts.

"It's not by chance that I come by Cowichan!" McGinty shouted at the stars.

He baited his hooks with canned mackerel from the Grand Banks, and trolled as the sun came up. He hauled a Spring salmon into his little dory.

"This one's for my darlin' Molly. It's as big and shiny as a codfish!" he cried. He hauled in another and another. "Hold on there, McGinty!"

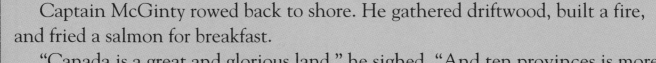

Captain McGinty rowed back to shore. He gathered driftwood, built a fire, and fried a salmon for breakfast.

"Canada is a great and glorious land," he sighed, "And ten provinces is more than ten inches!" Then he sang a new song: *"Oh, Bri-tish Co-lum-bia!"*

The song sounded out of tune.

Captain McGinty knelt down at the water's edge and emptied the water of the Atlantic Ocean into the water of the Pacific Ocean. Then he belted out a prayer of hope for the fish of Newfoundland.

That prayer blew with the westerly winds across the Strait of Georgia, over the Fraser Canyon, bobbed and bounced through the Rocky Mountains, up and over the ripples of the Alberta foothills, across the Prairies to Toronto, where it was blown off course to Ottawa, then, shooting down the roiling rivers of Quebec, sailed straight on, jiggity jig, all the way to Newfoundland.

"Hold on!" whispered McGinty.